I0570529

Blind

from the author of
Of Moths & Butterflies, Cry of the Peacock, Gods & Monsters
and
Absinthe Moon

Captive Press Publishing
Eden, NC

Copyright © 2012 V.R. Christensen
All rights reserved.
The Steam Powered Pocket Watch is published in cooperation with Literary Underground.

This is a work of fiction. Any similarities to persons living or dead are purely coincidental.

Cover design by V.R. Christensen.

Illustrations by B. Lloyd.

For more information about the author, see About the Author at the back of this book, or visit her website at www.VRChristensen.com

For more information about the artist, see the About the Illustrator page, or visit her website at www.wix.com/artscribe/paintings.

ISBN: 0615598005
ISBN - 13: 978-0615598000

Library of Congress Control Number: 2012908005

What people are saying about

Blind

"V.R. Christensen has created a beautifully written parable of Victorian life and the best and the worst it had to offer."
M. Louisa Locke, bestselling author of *Maids of Misfortune* and *Uneasy Spirits*

~

"Startling, surprising, mysterious and poignant, a tale to capture the imagination."
Rebecca Lochlann, author of *The Year-god's Daughter* and *The Thinara King*

~

"Magnificently written and thought provoking."
Crystal Schall*, reviewer for *The Book Rack

Acknowledgements

Vickie Irwin, M. Louisa Locke, Cheri Lasota, Rebecca Lochlann, Louise Galvin, B. Lloyd, Gev Sweeney, Laura Valetine Rosenlund, Tonya Lamm, Jenny Baxter, Rowenna Hamper Miller, anyone and everyone I may have momentarily forgotten,
Thank you!

Blind

Blind

It is an undeniable irony of life that, despite his many blessings, man is an ungrateful brute, finding handicaps and obstacles in those things which ought to bless him. The wealthy man, comfortable in his great house, with his soft furnishings and glowing hearth, is rarely sympathetic to the plight of the poor. If a man wants for food and raiment, ought he not to work for it? There are jobs enough for those who truly want them, declares our man of wealth and wisdom—from the chair he has not left all day.

Even modern conveniences become a source of irritation when they fail us in their obligations. We have employed them, paid good money for them, ought they not to work as they were designed to do?

The weather, as mundane a thing as can be imagined, yet manages to vex our lives as few other things can. The sun that makes it possible to grow our vegetable gardens and to take our jaunts to seaside towns, is often too glaring or too warm. Conversely, the rain that waters the crops, that fills the rivers and streams, ruins our plans and dampens our moods.

Our five senses, likewise, are blessings of which we are rarely mindful, save when we cannot use them to their best advantage. We curse our noses for the colds they catch, our hands for the injuries they suffer, our ears for the sounds that annoy us. The seeing man is often blinded to the subtleties of his surroundings by the obvious. He takes what he sees as truth and rejects what might lie beneath the surface. A beautiful house is more desirable than a humble one, however inconvenient it may be; a beautiful woman, likewise, far more suitable than she

1

who, though clever and resourceful, has less to be proud of in her appearance.

Those five senses (though some may argue six), while so essential to our lives, are things we too often take for granted. Is it possible that one, being deprived of a part of his natural senses, might appreciate all the more those that remain to him? Might he have a sweeter understanding of life and its hidden meanings?

Perhaps.

Perhaps not.

*　*　*

In a large suite of rooms in a sprawling country house sits such a man as we might put these questions to. At the moment we join him we see that our young friend is annoyed to distraction by the apparent lack of urgency conveyed by the pulling of the cord to the bells that are attached at its furthest end. In short, his servants are too slow. But this is only a part (though admittedly the greater part) of his anxieties. Other considerations circumstantially have added to them, for the weather, too hot yesterday, is dreary and damp today. A strange dog has found its way onto the property and will not leave off barking. His ears are ringing and his head has begun to ache. His tea, now tepid, has too much lemon. And on top of all this, he suspects he is coming down with a cold.

He rings the bell once more.

As to his sight, he cannot complain. That is, he has no new complaint to speak of. Arthur Tremonton was born, to his mother's sorrow and his father's indignation, blind.

*　*　*

By his staff, Arthur might have been described—were you to ask them, and assuming they were inclined to oblige—as a young man of better than average looks. His hair was fair and grew thick upon his head. His eyes bore no evidence of his malady save in their unusual paleness, a liquid blue that appeared almost white. He was tall, lithe and elegant, well dressed, well groomed and immaculate in speech if not entirely in manner. And, perhaps most significantly of all, he was well educated, which was an extraordinary thing considering he had never had a single day of school. No, he had lived his life in this house, confined almost exclusively (at first by the dictates of his parents, now dead, and then by habit) to an upper suite of rooms. He had been provided with tutors, naturally, but it was not until he had inherited his father's library, and the vast collection of books within it, that his education ventured toward anything nearing extraordinary. The deficiencies consequent of an education directed by a too protective mother and an unsympathetic father were more than made up for in the years that followed their passing.

Of course it was not the library alone Arthur had inherited, but the house, as well as its sprawling park, its ample staff, and even, to his great fortune, his father's aged valet, who had also served these many years as his teacher. Arthur could not read, but he could hear and he could remember and he could understand like few others. He possessed an almost supernatural gift of recollection, a keen com-prehension of concepts, histories, theories, and philosophies he could only experience in his mind. It was certainly a fortunate thing that Arthur had been born to money and position, for, at the age of seven and twenty, he could apply himself to no more practical occupation than that of perpetual scholar. He had no skills to speak of that were not of the cerebral persuasion. Had he been born a poor man—a mill worker, or a printer, a farmer, perhaps—he would have been at the mercy of an unforgiving world. What hardships he would have had to endure! He could not imagine it. But then he never tried. A man's hardships were his own business. Arthur Tremonton had his trials, and they were quite enough.

Where was Mrs. Pritchett with his tea? He rang the bell a third time. Or was it four? No matter.

Some, he knew, made themselves burdensome, and with far less reason than Arthur possessed. And yet hadn't *he* made something of his life?

Again, he applied his hand to the bell cord. Harder this time. Surely it was working well enough.

He would not make a nuisance of himself for the world! Such were better off dead. He would bother no one by his infirmity. And he would prefer that the consideration be reciprocated. He needed no one, which was perhaps a good thing as he had no friends. He did not like visitors and de-tested interruptions of all kinds. Most, by now, had learned to leave him in peace. Most, but not all. For those *infernal* charity Sisters would persist! And *why* must they keep coming? Their efforts were wasted; whether to extract money, or to plumb the depths of his soul. They could not help him, and he certainly did not want their pity.

3

Mrs. Pritchett at long last! She entered, freshened his cup, exchanged the pot, and quickly left once more, dismissed with a terse and impatient wave of her employer's hand.

Was Arthur lonely? Well, yes. Of course he was. But he valued his privacy and solitude more than he did company. And those who had ever come could never keep up a satisfactory conversation, for they could not compete with his intellect and only spoke of the things they saw and the places they went, as if they meant to brag of the talents they possessed and of which he had been born deficient. It was, in truth, nothing more than an insult to his impairment. He was blind! Was he ever going to cease to be blind? No! Would he ever be able to embark upon such adventures on his own? Of course not! So what use was there in discussing them? Try as a man might, Arthur could not be made to understand what a banana tree looked like, or an elephant, or the ocean. The phrases 'large as a house', 'fast as a horse', 'grey as the sea'... these meant nothing to him. One cannot comprehend the size and shape of a whale if one has not seen it for oneself. One cannot describe the shades of the dusk-lit sky if one has never seen color or shade or even vast and open space. It is impossible. And it is insulting! And he made it a point to tell them so.

Wisely, and mercifully, these visitors had ceased over time to come at all. All but the wretched, annoying, supercilious young women of the Sisters' Charitable Aid Society! They would come this very afternoon, despite a grumbling sky and the rain that tapped at the windows. They would come. They always came when he wished most to be left alone.

Just see if they didn't!

* * *

And they did come, just as foreseen. Arthur might have been accused by some of possessing the gift of clairvoyance, a sort of spiritual eye in place of the physical, but he would have denied it. He did not believe in such things. Such were for the weak of mind and palsied of intellect.

"What do they want today, Thompson?" Arthur de-manded of his valet upon the announcement of the unwanted guests.

"The usual, sir," the old man answered. "To know if you are in need of anything and in what way they might be of assistance to you."

"Haven't I told them before that I have no need of their 'assis-tance'?"

4

"You have, sir."

"Is there no getting rid of them?"

"I did tell them you were not receiving, but then you are never receiving. They were quite insistent."

Arthur drummed on the arm of his chair and remained this way, staring with unseeing but narrowed eyes and saying nothing at all for some time.

Thompson at last cleared his throat. "Might I remind you, sir, that both the Rector and the Squire are patrons? It might behoove you to—"

"Send them up, then. If they will not go until I have received them, then I suppose there is nothing for it but to receive them. Perhaps I can convince them their trouble is not worth the sacrifice to the comfort of either party."

"But, sir, I do not think—"

"Send them up, I say!"

And so Thompson quit the room, to return a few minutes later with the Sisters in tow. He announced them, but Arthur offered no welcome, no greeting of any kind.

"We beg your pardon, sir, for the intrusion," one of them said, breaking the silence.

"It *is* an intrusion, but then I believe you knew that when you forced your way in, so what use is there in apologizing? Your names?"

"Adair, sir. Rebecca Adair. And my companion is Miss Adelaide Hilton."

"Miss Hilton," he said very loudly, for he could feel her fear and wished to make his point as quickly and with as little effort as possible, "what excuse have you to give for badgering a man until he has no choice but to admit strangers into his private rooms?"

He heard a slight shuffle, as if she had taken a step or two back, toward the door in which she had so recently entered.

"Well?"

"She is mute, sir," said the first woman.

"Mute? And deaf, too, I suppose you'll tell me."

"No, sir. Her hearing is quite perfect. Perhaps unnaturally keen."

"Is that so? Well my hearing is just as keen, and I know, by the sound of her rustling skirts and uneasy feet, that she is any minute going to bolt from the room. Why do you wait? Be gone with you!" he said and threw a menacing wave of his arm toward the door.

Obediently, she ran from the room.

"And do not enter this house again or I'll set my dogs upon you!"

"That was unkind. And you have no dogs. You lied."

"Cannot you hear them? I don't know that either of you, or both, won't be torn to shreds this very morning."

"You have no dogs. The dog that barks is a stray and has no reason to protect you or your interests. I'm surprised at you, sir. I should think you, of all people, would know better than to take advantage of another's weaknesses."

"And do you have no weaknesses of your own, Miss Adair?"

"Certainly, I do, but I'd be a fool to confess them to the likes of you."

"Oh, it's the 'likes' of me now, is it? And I thought you'd come to offer aid."

"I'm not sure you require any. At least I no longer believe you deserve it."

"And who are you, *Miss* Adair, to be casting such judgments, and of your betters no less? Is this what you have been taught at the Sisters' Charitable Aid Society?"

"I beg your pardon, sir. We're from the Sisters' Benevolent Society for the Relief and Succor of the Blind and Otherwise Afflicted."

"The Sisters' Benevolent ... what?"

"The Sisters' Benevolent Society for the—"

"I heard you! And what relief do you think you can possibly offer me, I'd like to know! Have you some magic cure? Some divine gift of healing, perhaps?"

No answer was offered for this.

"What exactly is your purpose in coming? Do you mind telling me that?"

"I'm not sure I know, sir. I thought perhaps I might be of some use to you. I can see now that what you require is far greater than I alone can provide."

"There is nothing you can do for me, save to leave me be! Now good day to you."

"You are in need of something, though," the young wo-man replied. "Perhaps what you need is someone more like yourself in circumstance. I might send a Brother, instead."

"There is a Fraternal Brotherhood of Charitable Aid, I suppose?"

"No, sir. Not for the general public, that is. But I think one might make a special arrangement for someone in your particular need."

"I do not want your help, nor anyone's, Miss Adair. Are you slow of learning?"

"No, sir."

"Are you plain?"

She was silent for a moment, as if confused by the question. Or troubled by it. What, after all, had her appearance to do with the question at hand? "In a matter of speaking, sir, I suppose I am."

"I do not want any help from a plain-faced waif. If you were pretty, we might have something to discuss. As it is you are wasting my time. Good day to you."

"If you cannot see me, what can it matter what I—"

"Go away, and don't return! I do not want you, nor any of your sanctimonious charity 'Sisters'. Now go! And you can tell the rest of them I said so."

A long silence followed this. "Good day to you, sir," the girl said at last. "I will convey your message to the Sisters. In the meantime, I know of a Brother who might be glad to know of you."

"Did you not understand me, Miss Adair? I do not want your help."

All was silent, save the swishing of skirts and the light padding of feet on the floor. The occasional creak in the floor-boards.

"Did you hear me, Miss Adair?"

The click of the door closing.

"Miss Adair!"

And nothing more.

* * *

A slight and gloved hand rapped once more at a large oaken door. This time it was not to a grand manor house Rebecca sought entrance but a humble farmhouse. It was slow to be answered. Still slower to open. It groaned on its hinges as the man, Farmer Bentlow, groaned in tandem.

"What'd'ye want, now?" He asked the question without looking at her, and turned with the unspoken invitation to follow. It seemed he knew better than to argue over the matter of admittance.

She followed him into the kitchen, where he reclaimed his seat in a rickety chair beside that of his wife, who sat smoking a pipe.

"Tea's on," she said. "Will'ye have some?"

She knew better than to accept, laced as it too often was with rum. The charity Sisters were of no specific denomination, but they were teetotalers all. "No, thank you, ma'am."

"Won't ye make yourself comfortable?" was the question posed to her now, yet there were no other chairs in the room, and there was no one to get one for her. At least no one was prepared to do it.

She turned at the sound of whispering and shuffling. A sniff and what sounded like a choked sob, as if someone had lately been crying and had just recently left off. The sight was familiar enough to her. She had once been a child very like these, until rescued by the Sisters: a group of women, and sometimes men, who had come together for the betterment of the young and in need. Now she repaid their kindness by going door to door, keeping her eyes open for the mistreated of those they had placed, always looking for better situations, if there were any. There were rarely any. She'd seen worse than this, though. Had known worse herself. Much, much worse.

In a far corner, a young boy turned a mangle, as two young girls twisted and wrung the water from some newly laundered clothes. Their hands were bright red from the water and rough from so many months of hard work. The girl sniffed again, and looked at her from the corner of a red and swelling eye. Her hair was matted, her feet bare, her clothes wet and ragged. The other girl kept her head down, hard at work. The boy whispered occasional words of comfort to his adopted sisters, but he never stopped turning the mangle. Another girl entered with an empty basket, and filled it with the freshly wrung laundry before leaving again with a cur-sory look, and then a second, more uncertain one as she went outside to hang the washing on the line.

"I've come to see Zachary," Rebecca said, at last announcing her business.

"He ain't here," said the old man gruffly, and, taking the pipe from his wife's mouth, put it into his own. She did not seem to notice.

"Where might I find him?"

"He's up the way at Squire Humphrey's."

"Squire Humphrey's?" she asked in surprise. "He's given him employment?"

"Employment! As if readin' and discussin' and sittin' can be called work."

"He pays him, surely."

"Oh, he pays 'im right enough," the man answered and patted his waistcoat as a sly smile spread across his face.

"His learning has done him good, then. I'm glad of it. He has used his time wisely."

"His time? *His* time?" the woman said indignantly. "It ain't his time a'tall, not while he's livin' here."

"And on whose time is he when he goes to Squire Humphrey's?" Rebecca asked.

"As the Squire pays for it, I reckon it's his," Farmer Bent-low answered and patted his waistcoat again, this time hard enough to make the coins clink together. They would not remain there long. Farmer Bentlow had plans for the money already, she could tell by the gleam in his eye and the hungry way he licked his lips as he prepared to put the pipe back in his mouth. "He has to see to his other chores first, of course."

"He has a great deal of work to do," Rebecca observed aloud. "How does he manage it all?"

Mistress Bentlow shrugged. "He works twice, p'raps thrice as fast as any that have come afore or since, and so he's got more time to give the Squire, which is just as well." She examined Rebecca a moment, then looked away quickly, as if she'd forgotten the hazard in that occupation. "Don't s'pose you got any more like'im. We could use a few more like'im. Not like that riff raff we got last time," she said with a jerk of her head in the direction of the laundry waifs.

"There are no more like him," Rebecca answered quite simply, though there might have been more yet to glean from her words than the farmer and his good wife were ever likely to comprehend.

"Hmm!" the woman said in apparent disappointment. "Ye didn't bring the mute girl with ye?" she observed with a glance where Miss Hilton ought to have stood.

"I'm afraid she wouldn't come again, Mistress Bentlow, not after the last time."

"How's I s'posed to know she didn't talk 'cause she could-n't?"

"I did tell you so."

"Nine times out'a ten a child like that's just stubborn. Sometimes a little encouragement with a heavy stick will cure 'em."

"Like it did for Zachary? Though I think what you dealt him could hardly be called a 'little' encouragement, whatever the kind. You're lucky you didn't kill him."

"Say what you will. It worked didn'it?"

"Such a cure won't help Miss Hilton. I'm afraid the Sisters won't be sending any more children to you."

Mistress Bentlow took a quick glance toward the red-eyed laundress. "Well...," she said and slowly. "Who's to say we won't make another Zachary out of one of 'em yet."

"Zachary is a man of his own making, Mrs. Bentlow. I think anyone can see that."

"I, for one, don't see what the fuss is about," Farmer Bent-low exclaimed and tapped the ashes out of his pipe and into the hearth. "He's an ox, and make no mistake. I suppose I ought to give him some credit for being half blind, but aside from that, he ain't much. I suppose a girl like ye'd think he's something, at least to look at." And he laughed, nudging his wife, who made a poor job of hiding her amusement in her tea cup. Mr. Bentlow took no such consideration.

Handsome as he was, she did make much of him, for he was far better than the circumstances in which he had been placed and raised should have allowed, but she did not wish to say so. "I've not come of my own accord, Farmer Bentlow. The Sisterhood has found him a position."

"Are you deaf, too, girl? I just told ye he's got a position!"

"Yes. And I'm glad of it. But I think I ought to tell him, at all events. It's a good position, and I think he'll not regret it, despite Squire Humphrey's kindness."

"You mean to take him from us, do ye? Well I'll not let him go!" the old woman cried. "Not for all the money in the world!"

"He's a grown man, nearly twenty," Rebecca answered. "He's long been of an age where he can make those decisions for himself. That he's stayed with you as long as he has is a testament to his sense of gratitude, but it can't last forever. It's time he chose his own way, whether it's taking a more per-manent position with Squire Humphrey, or venturing out to see what other opportunities might be available to him."

"Like this one ye've come to tell him of?"

"Perhaps."

"Well, as I said, he ain't here."

"I'll wait."

Farmer Bentlow, with a menacing look, stood from his chair, nearly knocking it to the ground. "Then you're not welcome!"

"As you say," she answered and stood. "Good day to you both." She bowed before turning from the cottage and the misery that inhabited it.

* * *

10

On the road to Hurtfew farm she found him. Dusk was nearly spent and the unlit path was heavily cloaked in shadow by the time he appeared. The sky had clouded over, but the night was warm and the evening pleasant. At last she heard his heavy footsteps on the path, and the whistling of a tuneless melody. A memory, perhaps, from an earlier time. A time before the world had been silenced to him.

She waited until he was quite near before she showed herself. There was no use calling. He would never hear her. Neither was his eyesight very good. It was better than it had been when he had first come to the Bentlows. He was a blind boy then, but they'd put him to work anyway. He'd received some rather hard punishment when he had upset a teacup, and the result was a concussion and the loss of his hearing. But, oddly, one eye had regained its sight.

She entered the path. He held the lamp forward to see who it was that had stopped him. He examined her cloaked figure and she drew off her hood so he might see her face. His look of recognition was paired with one of pleasant surprise. The way he observed her, unflinchingly, was so rare she was tempted to retreat back into the shadows of her hooded cloak. Or perhaps bask in the warmth of it. She never knew quite what to do before those pale blue eyes that both could and could not see.

"I was just thinking of you," he said. "And here you are."

"Here I am."

"Have you been waiting long?" he asked, with a glance toward the fallen tree where she had been resting, but returned his gaze to her face almost immediately. He could only understand her by watching her mouth. He had learned to recognize the shapes of words on a person's lips, and so long as that person stood just before him, with good light, it was almost as if he were not deaf at all.

"Not long," she answered.

Despite his weakened sight, he was good at seeing through her deceptions. Not that there had ever been many between them, but if she told a little lie now and again for his comfort, she saw nothing wrong with it. He, perhaps, might not have agreed.

"And what good fortune has brought you my way to-night?" he asked her.

"I have some news, but I was warned by Farmer Bentlow you might not want it."

"I'd like to know it anyway."

"I've found a position for you. With a gentleman. He is blind like you. Or, rather, like you once were."

"I have a position already, and I'm rather fond of it."

"Squire Humphrey has been good to you."

"He has, indeed."

"But the money you would make from Mr. Tremonton would be yours to keep. And you'd have a roof over your head, and a room to yourself."

"Sounds lonely."

She felt her face grow warm. "I'd like you at least to meet him," she answered.

"If you really wish it, but if Squire Humphrey didn't pay me at all, I'd still hate to leave him. He's taught me to read, to speak as you hear me, almost as a gentleman, to play the piano. He thinks I ought to learn to sing."

"To play? And sing, too? Is it possible? How ever do you hear the music?"

"I can feel it. It's the oddest thing. Like a memory. I wish you could hear it." He laughed. "For that matter, I wish *I* could hear it." He seemed then to have struck upon an idea. "You might come, you know, to pay a visit there. To hear me play. You might do that thing you do."

"I might," she said and smiled.

Now it was his turn to blush. He had never asked before, and he was always embarrassed by any selfish desire he expressed for himself. He had survived, thrived in fact, by dedicating his life to the service of others. An instrument in the hands of He who some might say had cursed him.

She removed her glove.

"You needn't," he said. "I should never have suggested it."

She raised her naked hand, but he stopped it with his own.

"Now," she said, and turned from him, "it is my gift and I'll give it where I like."

She turned to him again and raised her hand once more. He did not attempt to stop her this time, but looked a little abashed, never-theless. She laid that hand, very gently on his cheek, and held it there.

He exhaled and looked at her. Waiting. And then his face came alight as he began to look all around him, searching for the source of what he could not see but could now hear. The nightingales were out and singing loudly. There were crickets, too, and even she wondered, as she watched him won-der, how it was she could ever have taken so much night song for granted.

At last his eyes rested once more on her face. "Thank you," he said, but she knew he had not had enough. It was all, perhaps more than, he thought he deserved.

"It makes me happy when I can use it so," she answered him. And it was no lie.

As if in a gesture of reciprocal gratitude, he lifted his hand to her face and touched his fingers to the scar that ran a long and ragged line from her hairline, over one eyelid, down her cheek and very nearly to her chin.

"It seems to fade more every time I see you," he said.

"Your eyesight doesn't improve," she teased.

"It improves enough to see what needs to be seen," he said, apparently content with the fact. "It's a pity you cannot use your gift to heal yourself. Though I suspect the injury is more within than with-out."

She flushed once more in the lamplight and busied herself with the glove she had just put back on.

"I'm sorry. I should not have said that."

"It may be true, after all."

"But I can only guess what you must have suffered. I fear I dredge up memories best forgotten. Forgive me."

"There is nothing to forgive," she said, and turned to take his arm.

"Are you walking me home now?" he asked.

"I can hear Mrs. Bentlow calling you. It's a good thing, perhaps, that you had me stop when I did. It'd be no blessing to hear *her* voice."

"Yes, and I'll be in for it, if I don't hurry."

"Well, then," she said, "we shall hurry."

And so they did, speaking no more until they came to the fork that split off in one direction toward Bentlow Farm, and in the other to the Society house where she spent every night.

"You will remember what I said?" she asked him.

"You really want me to meet this fellow?"

"I do."

"Then I will, if you insist. I can't promise more than that. I don't know how I'll get leave from the farm, even for a day."

"Leave that to me."

He examined her dubiously, and then, perhaps seeing something in her resolve, or possibly knowing by her past successes that she was a woman to accomplish her purposes, he relented.

13

"Very well," he said. "I'll trust you to it. Are you all right to walk on your own? I hate to leave you."

"I'm safe, thank you, Mr. Goodfellow. Good night."

"Goodnight, Miss Adair."

She watched for a moment as he walked on. Watched, until the scene was no longer so pleasant. She turned her back upon Bentlow farm.

"And where have you been?" Mrs. Bentlow was heard to say through the growing darkness. "What's taken you so long? And where is it? Hand it over."

The faint clink of coins was heard, and nothing more. Mrs. Bentlow was thus easily placated. And in a quarter of an hour, Mr. Bentlow might have been seen by any idle observer to leave the cottage for the nearest alehouse, not to return again until early morning light.

But by then, Rebecca would be safe, and nearly snug in the bed she shared with Adelaide. The girl who never spoke, save in her sleep. The poor girl's screams and night terrors were only abated by Rebecca's proximity. Zachary might find refuge from the Bentlows in the Squire, but Rebecca *was* the refuge for some. There was no escaping that, even if she wanted to. And there was only one reason, a very selfish reason, to think of it.

* * *

"So you have returned," Arthur Tremonton said as Rebecca stood once more before him.

"I have, sir."

"And where is your companion?"

"She could not attend me today. And I felt, in light of our last visit, that perhaps she ought not to come again. Not here." She did not add, because he would not care, or perhaps would find amusement (even pleasure) in the knowledge that Adelaide's nightmares had returned once more. Adelaide called them visions, scenes from past episodes in the lives of those whom she met in her work. It was not Arthur Tremonton who had scared her off, but the house and the memories it held.

"You did not feel it unwise to come alone?" he asked her.

"Am I in some danger of you, sir?"

He laughed. "Your business then, if you please."

"Do you have family, Mr. Tremonton?"

"Family?"

"Yes. Family. Your parents are deceased, I know that, but is there no one else?"

"I have an uncle who has never spoken to me and an aunt who considers my affliction a curse on the Tremonton name. Is that the sort of thing you mean?"

"You have no sisters?"

"None, Miss Adair."

"No brothers?"

Silence.

"Do you not wish for some companionship? Someone in whom you might confide, who might share, or possibly ease your burdens?"

"And what burdens might those be, Miss Adair?"

"We all bear burdens, Mr. Tremonton. From the greatest to the least of us, we all bear burdens. Would yours not be eased by some companionship?"

Mr. Tremonton leaned back in his chair and rubbed at his chin. After a moment of contemplation, he rose and approached her, his blind eyes wandering the space before him, concentrating on the occupation of hearing rather than the sight he did not possess. He stopped just before her. "You believe I'm in need of companionship, do you?"

"I do, sir."

He seemed to consider for a moment, and then, raising his hand, he placed it on her unscarred cheek. He felt her face, her nose, the shape of her brow, the outline of her mouth and chin. He smiled, satisfied with his findings.

"Are you applying for the job yourself, then, Miss Adair? Because I just might consider it."

With her ungloved hand, she slapped him hard across the face.

He half turned with the force of it. But when he turned to her again, his eyes were on her, on her face, focused there. In his look was surprise, wonder, then confusion and at last fear as the focus once more faded from his gaze.

"What in the *devil's* name was that? What did you just do to me?"

"I taught you a lesson, Mr. Tremonton, about how to talk to a lady."

"You, a lady?" He scoffed, then looked once more alarm-ed. Desperate. "Tell me what you did. Tell me how you did it! Are you some witch?"

"I'm not a witch, Mr. Tremonton."

"And what happened to your face?"

There was silence then, as his blind gaze dropped from that spot where an ill healed injury marked the only im-perfection in her appearance.

"Can you do it again?"

She took a silent step away from him.

He reached out a hand to touch her, to lay hold of her if he could, but there was only thin air before him. Focused as he now was on the sight he did not have, his hearing was no longer so attuned. "Do it again."

"So you can insult me? I think not."

"Your face... It's..."

"You were granted, for ten seconds, the gift of sight, and that's what you saw? My face? And how it did not please you?"

He was silent for a moment, thoughtful, and then: "What happened to you?"

"Tell me about your father, Mr. Tremonton."

"My father is none of your concern."

"Did he disown you? Did he cast you aside because of your affliction? Did he reject you?"

"I said it's none of your concern!"

"And your mother?"

"We do not speak of her. I– I do not speak of her."

"Did she reject you, too? Or was it that your father rejected her, as well?"

"No! ... It was she who rejected him! By her disloyalty! By her betrayal of him. And of me. If she had to go, it was her own fault. She had shamed us."

"She was cast off because she was unfaithful to your father? Are you certain? Or was it for no other reason than that he could not accept the fact that he sired an unsighted child?"

"How dare you!"

"Your mother died in this house."

"Get out!"

"Did she kill herself? Is that what happened?"

"Get out, I say!"

"I have someone I'd like you to meet, Mr. Tremonton. A companion for you. Someone to keep you company."

"I don't need any company. I've told you so already!"

"I mean to bring him here. I think there is much you might learn from him. He is blind like you. Or was."

16

"Was?"

"A fortunate accident restored the sight in one eye."

The look on Mr. Tremonton's face was at once hungry and appalled. "You? Did you do it? Are you responsible?"

"I had nothing to do with it. My talents only go so far as a man's faith will allow. Yours is particularly weak."

He considered this a moment, and then: "You did not tell me what happened to you." He nodded and looked, for the moment, a little sick as he recalled the gruesome scar.

"My story won't inspire in you any sympathy, so I think I'll leave it for you to think about. I'll return. In a day or two."

"You insist on bringing this...this...person, into my home when I've expressly forbidden you to do it?"

"I think I must."

"Why? What is it you hope to achieve?"

"I mean for you to see a bit of yourself, Mr. Tremonton. Or what you might be. I mean to open your eyes."

"What does that mean?" He looked a little frightened.

She offered no answer, yet still he waited for one. At last he took another step toward her, but she anticipated him, and quietly as before, she took a step back, and then another and another, until she was nearly across the room.

"Don't go! Not yet."

She waited in silence for him to explain himself. What did he want of her? She didn't need to ask, only to wait. She knew the answer already.

"Will you do it again? What you did before? Can you make me see for good?"

"As I said, Mr. Tremonton, you need faith for that. You haven't any. Not yet. You might in time. But not yet."

"Faith in what?"

"Good day to you, Mr. Tremonton."

"Wait! Come back. Come back, I say!"

But she was gone and walking, nearly running down the stairs and out of the house. The door was opened for her by a surprised valet, and was shut again with a scrape and a thud. She didn't look back. She never looked back. It was a rule she had set for herself long ago, and today, especially, she would keep it.

* * *

17

Another door. Another knocker, yet here there was no waiting. There were no ill looks, no impatient or unwell-coming words as the man opened the door. There was no fear, no disgust, no prejudice of any kind.

"Welcome, Miss Adair," the man said. "If you'll just wait here a moment, I'm sure the Squire will be happy to see you."

He gestured toward a chair by the fire. She took it and made herself quite comfortable. But she had not been seated more than five minutes when Squire Humphrey entered.

"My dear Miss Adair, what brings you here? It's such a rare pleasure, you know. It's been some time since I made a donation. One moment and I'll get something for you."

"Thank you, no, Squire Humphrey. That's not why I came. I only wanted to speak with you, to ask you, in fact, how Mr. Goodfellow gets on."

He looked pleased by the aspect of what was very nearly a social call. He puffed himself up and patted his protruding belly. "Well, if you'll stay for tea, we can discuss it."

"I'd like that," she answered with a grateful smile.

Squire Humphrey led her into his best parlor, where they awaited the tea that was not long in coming.

"Your companion has not come with you today. How does Miss Adelaide get on?"

"She is worse, I'm afraid. She was recently given quite a scare, and I'm afraid her nightmares have returned in earnest. In part that's why I've come."

"Oh?"

"That is, it is indirectly related to Mr. Goodfellow."

"Our Zachary?"

She nodded, but was not sure how to go on from there. "In a way, though very round about. I am grateful for all you've done for him, sir. It's so much more than anyone else has ever done. The Sisters are very grateful." She blew on her tea, took a sip and then set it down. "*I* am very grateful."

"Yes, my dear, and I know it," the Squire answered. "But the boy has real talent, as you well know, and I think you would agree with me that it would be a sin to let it go to waste."

"I'm afraid not many would take your view. The talent you see in him, the potential, not many would take the trouble to look for it."

18

"People are afraid of what they do not understand. A boy like Zachary..." He shook his head. "They're most often despaired of, discarded. What his life might have been if the Sisters had not found him. Many a man could make an example of that boy's life. If I had half his determination..." he said and did not finish, but seemed to grow thoughtful. He tugged at one side of his forked beard until it was a good two inches longer than the other. "Well, well," he said at last, "I dare say you didn't come to talk about my shortcomings."

"Actually, I wanted your opinion. And your counsel, if you will give it."

"Of course, my dear. If I can."

"The truth is, Squire Humphrey, that something has turned up, an opportunity that I do not think he should miss out on, though it will take him away from you. If only for a time."

Squire Humphrey's brow rose thoughtfully. It was clear the prospect was not a pleasing one to him, but he was prepared to hear her out nevertheless.

"There is a gentleman, not many miles away, who is in need of a companion. Not any companion, but one whose condition is very nearly like his own."

"You are speaking of Arthur Tremonton, I take it."

"Indeed, I am," she answered."

"I knew his mother, you know."

Rebecca was very rarely taken by surprise. She was rendered nearly speechless by this. "Will you tell me..." she said at last. "Will you tell me about her?"

"Why the sudden interest in Arthur Tremonton?" he asked with a look that hinted at suspicion. Did he think her prying, or did he wonder at her motives?

"He has been an object of interest to me for some time," she attempted to explain. "I think he might benefit by meeting someone so very like him in situation. Someone, in fact, whose circumstances are far worse, and yet who has made a better go of his life than he has done."

"Do you really think Tremonton will see it that way?"

"I intend that he should."

Squire Humphrey thought a long while. And then: "You want to know about Mrs. Tremonton?"

"Yes, sir. I do."

He sat back and sighed heavily. He looked, it seemed, a little sad as he prepared himself to tell the tale. "Evelyn Tremonton was a good woman. The best, the loveliest I ever knew, both in temperament and appearance. In fact you might say I—"

"You loved her," Rebecca presumed, having come to the conclusion by the warmth in his tone, and by the look in his eye that spoke of loss.

"I did," he answered, "but we were friends and she could not consider me as anything more. She chose Tremonton, of course, and I knew she'd regret it. Despite his birth, his position, his wealth, he was no gentleman. They married. Not long after, they had a child. He was blind. Tremonton was incensed. It was her fault; he was certain of it. She had embarrassed him, shamed him, and he would have nothing more to do with her. She remained in the house, in private rooms. She lived a very quiet, lonely existence. Lonely except for her boy, whom she doted upon."

"She did not reject him?"

"No, my dear. She adored him. He was not then what he is now."

"No, of course not. Do go on."

"Years went by, and Tremonton spoke to his wife rarely, never sought her company, never forgave her. She was not permitted in the dining room, nor to receive guests. He locked the boy and his mother in a suite of upper rooms, and there they stayed, save for their daily walks in the remoter parts of the park, where no one could see them."

"No one but you."

"You are uncommonly perceptive, my dear." He smiled awkwardly and went on. "And then, by some miracle, she was found once more to be with child." Squire Humphrey blushed and looked at her askance. "Don't think it, my dear. I cared for her far too much to cause her any harm. And I knew it would. It did, in fact, despite her innocence. Tremonton grew aware of her condition. He waited and watched. It's possible he saw us together and formed the conclusion. Quite possibly he needed no evidence at all. But when the child was born, he too was found to be blind. Tremonton came unhinged. He declared that both the children were conceived in sin, and that their afflictions were God's curse on her shameful behavior."

"Was it true? Was it even possible?"

"It was not impossible, I suppose. A woman whose heart has been trammeled by such fetters as Robert Tremonton placed upon hers must find something to live for, however clandestine or dangerous."

"Do you believe it?"

"I don't," he said. "To my mind she was never of that make. But then love, as they say..." He was silent a time before continuing. "I went to school with Robert Tremonton. We were never what you'd call friends. But it was much talked about in the dormitories that as a boy he walked in his sleep. He would retire to his own bed and wake up, the next morning, in the most unexpected of places. Broom cupboards, the infirmary. He once awoke in the bed of one of the nurses who had spent the night away with family."

"He was a somnambulist?"

"He was so as a child."

"And as an adult?"

"I have no reason to doubt Evelyn's account. If he was so as a child, it is quite easy to suppose he was so as an adult. As a husband, even. And as a father, though he refused to acknowledge his off-spring."

"And she said so?"

"All but, my dear," he said and patted her hand. "There are stories no lady would ever tell, but I believe it with all my heart."

"And what became of her?"

"Once the child was dealt with, sent to the workhouse to starve or be worked to death—I doubt he gave it a thought—Tremonton began making arrangements to have her committed to a private asylum. He had no difficulty pro-viding the necessary evidence, for he'd provided for it. She was a recluse, though by his own insistence. She had blamed herself for the boy's malady... Well, isn't it always a woman's fault when a child is not quite all it should be? And who was to say, after all, with so much disappointment, so much wrong already done, that she might not harm her child to spite the man who had taken the other away? Tremonton went about making the arrangements. The doctors were sent for to perform their examinations, though it was no more than a matter of formality, for Tremonton had paid them well to carry out their jobs with expediency."

Squire Humphrey stopped here quite abruptly. He removed his spectacles and cleaned them with his napkin.

Rebecca laid a gloved hand upon his arm. "Do go on, sir. If you can."

He cleared his throat and replaced his glasses, then looked at her before nodding, a solemn smile upon his face.

"There is not much left to tell, I'm afraid. When Tremonton arrived home from the station, and with the doctors in tow, Evelyn was already dead. She had hanged herself from the library gasolier."

"Poor woman! And the child? The younger boy? What became of him?"

"I believe you already have your suspicions about that."

She did not answer. She only looked at him.

In turn, he examined her for a long time, pulling at his beard once more. "I like Zachary. I think you know that. I'm fond of him. Fond as if he were my own son. I do not want to see him hurt."

"I don't want that either."

He gave her a sideways glance and chuckled. "No. I believe you don't. And may I ask what you hope to achieve by this plan of yours? Arthur Tremonton cannot truly be looking for a companion."

"No, sir."

"And Zachary, unless I'm very much mistaken, is not anxious to look for a new position."

"No, sir."

"Then why, may I ask, are you doing this?"

"It is the only way... The only way he—Mr. Tremonton, I mean—I want him to see, to know that he might have lived his life to a higher, to a better purpose. I want him to understand that the affliction that affects his eyes ought to allow him to see things more clearly, not less."

"It isn't his blindness that prevents that, my dear."

"No. That's just my point. It is his anger, his resentment, his pride, his education, even. He is the blindest man I have ever known, while Zachary...he is..."

"The most clear sighted?"

"Yes," she said quite breathily.

"He has a gift for seeing things as they truly are, for believing where others would have given up hope, for finding happiness where any other man would have despaired."

"Yes," she said again, and in the same manner as before.

"And is there something in this for our dear boy?"

"I believe so," she answered more confidently. "But I cannot be quite certain what it is. Freedom, perhaps. A chance at the future he deserves. To tell you the truth, I'm not entirely certain. It depends, I think, on what it is he wants for himself."

For a moment they sat in silence, contemplating each other and the words they had each spoken. There was much to consider, much to hope for. And much to feel anxious about, as well. As the air settled around them, Rebecca gradually grew conscious of the strains of a piano being softly played in another room. She looked once more to Squire Humphrey. Who smiled.

"That, I believe, would be our dear boy now," he said with a smile as proud as any natural father's could be. "Go to him, do. I will join you shortly."

* * *

Rebecca entered alone and stood a moment to listen as gentle music filled the room. The melodies were not perfectly played; the timing and meter were slightly off. The pieces, fragments of them, were played consecutively, without rest. Some were well known, familiar refrains, which then drifted off into strange and unfamiliar melodies, to pick up again upon the familiar, or vaguely familiar, then dissolving once more into something else. It was as if all the music Zachary had ever heard, or ought to have heard, had been stored up inside him just waiting to be let out.

By degrees and with unconscious stealth, Rebecca approached the piano until she came to stand just behind him. She did not think what she did, but silently removed her gloves and placed her hands on each side of his head, running her bare fingers through his fair hair until they touched his ears.

He paused in his playing for just a moment, the last chord resonating, hanging in the air like the suspense she felt. Slowly he began to play again, tentatively then growing in confidence and making none of the mistakes she had heard—and that he had not—but a moment before. He played and played as the music filled the room and the house, as it grew louder and more impassioned. Until, at long last, Zachary stopped, breathless and seemingly exhausted. Yet he remained, his shoulders slumped, his head hanging low above the keys.

Rebecca removed her hands and took a step back falling into a nearby chair.

It was only then that Zachary turned to look at her, and her alone. To offer his unspoken gratitude. Had it been too much? Ought she to have asked his permission? There were tears pooling in his pale eyes, streaming down his face. Had she not been seated, she might have flown to him, pressed her lips to those beautiful eyes, blind or not. To his ears, deaf or hearing. But she did not move, just sat staring at him, receiving

23

what he silently offered across the impossible and uncertain distance that measured scarcely more than an arm's length.

The clearing of a throat broke the silence. Squire Humphrey stood within the door's frame. "You did say you would stay to dinner, did you not, Miss Adair?" he inquired of her.

She looked to him, blinking the tears from her own eyes. "I would like that, sir. Thank you."

"I'll just make the directions, then. I'll not be a moment." And he left the room again.

Rebecca turned back to Zachary, but he had turned back to the piano. Silence, then. Not so awkward, but awkward enough.

Rebecca rose and crossed to the bay window, where she looked out upon the sunlit garden, while Zachary plucked and plinked at the piano keys as if they were the scraps of a cold and tasteless dinner. Perhaps what she had given him was no gift at all. Perhaps what she possessed was the power to awaken a person to the consciousness of what they did not have. What was admirable or redeeming, or even helpful, in that?

She turned once more toward the room to find Zachary looking at her.

"I'm sorry," she said to him.

"You're sorry? Don't *you* be sorry. *I'm* sorry."

"Whatever for?"

"I'm sorry I have nothing to give you in return. If only I had something to offer you."

"I don't want anything from you, Mr. Goodfellow."

"No? I hope that's not true. I know very well you have no selfish desires, but there are times, like now, when I wish you did."

"You wish I were selfish?" she asked with a timorous laugh.

"I only wish you wanted something from me, and that I had the power to grant it. But it is ungentlemanly of me to speak so," he said and returned his attention to the piano before him. "No money," he said and hit a discordant note. "No property or position." He hit another. "No future." Another. "Nothing."

With each of those foul notes, she had taken a step nearer. She was close enough to touch him now, and she laid a hand upon his arm. "See Arthur Tremonton. Do that for me. It will be enough."

He did not look at her. With her hand still upon him, he didn't need to. He nodded his acquiescence.

* * *

24

The hours that passed before dinner did so in a sort of dazed preoc-cupation. Rebecca, thinking about the upcoming visit they were soon to pay on Mr. Tremonton, and what might—and might not—come of it, was not quite up to the ensuing conversation. It seemed evident that Squire Humphrey wished to exhibit Zachary's capabilities by displaying him in his usual capacity, as reading and conversational companion. The two men did seem quite at home in each other's company, and Rebecca felt a slight twinge of guilt that she was considering a scheme that might endanger this warm and easy, and for Zachary at least, highly beneficial, arrangement.

Rebecca was no better able to keep up with the conversation at dinner than she had been earlier, yet she found the easy atmosphere of Squire Humphrey's home, and of the company, relaxing. For the first time in a long while she had the opportunity of realizing just how tired she was, how exhausting life could be outside of these walls. Here no one judged her, no one frowned upon her appearance. Here she was absolutely and entirely safe. She found she did not want to leave, that she would like to stay forever. The fine meal, the warm fire, and the cozy atmosphere lulled her. She could fall asleep where she sat. Perhaps her desire was apparent. Or perhaps it was her yawning that inspired Squire Humphrey's invitation that she stay the night. He practically insisted upon it.

"I really couldn't," she objected. "I must get back to the Sisters to-night. I'm needed there. Adelaide, you know."

"Surely they can get by without you for one night," he argued. "Of course I can have the carriage brought out, if you insist. Though it hasn't been used in an age."

"Certainly not, sir. I never meant to be such a bother. I'll walk, of course."

"You'll do no such thing," Zachary intervened. "You'll be a good girl, and grateful, and accept Squire Humphrey's invitation. I'm sure a message can be sent, and someone else spared for Miss Adelaide's sake."

"I suppose so. Mrs. O'Reilly understands her case as well as I."

"Good," Zachary answered, "then it is settled." He looked up at the mantle clock then, just as it chimed the hour. The smile on his face faded and his brow knotted. "And I'm afraid I'll have to be on my way."

"Dear heaven, my boy, so you will. The Bentlows will be quite put out by your returning home at this hour."

"It's an easy price for such an evening's enjoyment as I've had," he answered as he rose from his chair. "But really I *had* best go."

Squire Humphrey and Rebecca walked with him as far as the entrance hall, where the squire said his goodbyes and left them. Rebecca followed Zachary out of doors, where they stood for a moment or two in silence.

"Goodnight, Zachary," she said at last. It was what she had come out to say, after all. So why was it so difficult to do?

He took her ungloved hand in his and placed it against his face. "Say it again."

She hesitated only a moment, and then: "Goodnight, Zachary."

He held her hand there a moment longer, then pressed it to his lips and released it. "I meant what I said, you know."

"And what was that? I'm afraid you'll have to remind me."

He considered a moment, and then answered with a question rather than a statement. "Is it true what you said? That you want nothing?"

She felt the heat rise in her face, but smiled in spite of it. "No," she answered.

He smiled, too, though somewhat regretfully, and remained a moment longer, just standing there, looking at her. But there was nothing more that could be said. Not now, at any rate. At last, and with a polite bow, he turned from her and from the Squire's home, to return to his own, where he would no doubt be berated for his late return, where his deficiencies would be exaggerated and his strength and goodness—Oh what goodness!—would be counted as naught.

For perhaps the last time.

* * *

The garret room was unusually cold. Adelaide's one source of heat (and comfort) had not come home tonight. She pulled her knees up tight to her chest and wrapped her arms around them for warmth. She would get little rest tonight, but the loss of sleep would be made up for by the absence of dreams. Those nightmares, thanks to Mr. Arthur Tremonton and his prison of a house, had begun again. But she would not wake the others tonight. She would not soil her bed nor her clothes. There would be no disturbances because she would not sleep. She would not.

If she listened carefully, through the still of the night and the rats nibbling and scratching within the walls, the breathing and occasional

snoring of her fellow charity Sisters, she could hear the regular chiming
of the great hall clock two floors below. It chimed every quarter hour,
just once for the first quarter, twice for the half hour and thrice for the
three quarter hour. In this way she marked off the night. But in time,
perhaps from cold, or boredom, or want of sleep, she grew confused.
She heard the half hour chime and then chime again. The scratching and
nibbling grew to clawing and champing. And then she thought she heard
a creaking upon the stairs. Perhaps Rebecca had returned, after all.

Comforted by this thought, and nearly desperate to find that it was
so (for she was excruciatingly tired) she rose. This great maze of a house
confused her even in the daylight hours, but at the landing at the top of
the stairwell she found that a door had been left open that had never
been left open before. Just inside the door was another staircase, to a
higher garret? Was that possible? She supposed so, for the house had
ever so many towers and upper rooms. She climbed the stairs a step or
two and stopped to allow her eyes to adjust to the darkness. At the top,
a light seemed to shine, perhaps through a window. She climbed another
step or two, but stopped again upon realizing that the light was no longer
stationary but approached her. She took a step back, nearly forgetting
the stair and stumbled. The light continued to approach. She stepped
down again, and then another, but stumbled once more and fell hard
upon the landing, knocking her head upon the open door and sending
that door crashing against the wall. She rubbed her head and blinked, but
the light was bearing down upon her now, and she could not quite rise
to her feet in time to escape it. Surely there was no need to be so
frightened. No doubt one of the matrons had only come to check on the
sleeping girls. To see, perhaps, who it was that was out of bed.

"Mrs. O'Reilly, is that you?" Adelaide asked.

There was no answer. The lantern remained, shining in her face, and
the confusion wrought by her inability to see anything else at last became
too disconcerting. She shoved the lamp aside, sending it crashing to the
ground, where it illuminated a pair of thick, black boots.

"Who is it?" she asked. The last flames of the lamp, now licking at
the spilled kerosene, glinted off an object in the man's hand as he held it
aloft. "Who are you? What do you want?" She heard the panic in her
voice and it frightened her all the more.

The glinting object moved, lowered, coming toward her, flashing
like lightning in the near darkness. A sliver of moonlight caught at its
jagged edges and reflected. It was a large shard of glass, held menacingly
in a gloved hand.

"What are you doing? What do you want!" she cried again. There was no answer. She scrambled backwards trying to get away, but she was not fast enough. The glass came at her again, cutting and slashing. She felt her face grow warm, as though something wet were spreading across her forehead, her eye, her cheek, her chin, then cooling in the night air. She reached up to feel it, slippery and warm, and to fight off the next blow. It came anyway. She tried once more to scramble to her feet, and had nearly gained her footing when she lost it again. The shard came at her, but missed. What offense had she caused Mr. Adair, that he should wish to destroy her? What harm had she done anyone? But she knew the answer. None. This was not her reality, but a nightmare. A vision from someone else's past. Could she escape it? She could only try. She was moving away from that glass dagger now. Not back, no, but down. Down and down and down. And then...peace.

* * *

After a night spent in a warm room in a soft bed, alone, and with no interruptions through the night, after a lovely dinner and a fine breakfast, after so much care and kindness, Rebecca found it terribly difficult to return to the charity house. Cold and dark it was, too. Even when it was filled with people, it felt empty. All the more so today, for there was no one about, and those who did linger, turned their backs on her and sniffed into their handkerchiefs, or glared at her with accusing stares. She did not understand it.

"What's going on, Mary?" she asked one of the girls. "Where is everyone?"

The girl only answered by looking up toward the staircase and the second floor.

With a sense of apprehension, Rebecca climbed the stairs. Only here there was no one, not a soul. The doors were all closed and the hallways empty, but then most of those who lived on this floor were hard at work at this hour. She climbed the next set of stairs to the third floor. Here a young girl sat on the hallway floor, her knees pulled up to her chest and rocking back and forth.

"Is something the matter?" she asked the girl. "Can I help you?"

The girl shook her head ferociously and kept rocking. Rebecca reached out a gloved hand to touch her, but the girl flinched and shied from her.

Reluctantly Rebecca left her. By now that feeling of faint apprehension had settled into something hard and cold and seemingly unbearable.

She climbed the next flight of stairs and arrived in the attic where the garret room she shared with half a dozen girls like (and not like) her was situated. She opened the door and found it would not open all the way, for someone stood against it. They moved as she pushed the door open wider.

"What is going on?" she asked, confused, and grew alarmed as she realised the throng had gathered around her bed. "Has something happened?"

Without a word, the crowd parted, to reveal a figure lying there, cloaked in a sheet and very still. As Rebecca came near, the sheet was lowered to reveal a death white face, mouth closed, blue lips pulled taught, and the most terrified look fixed upon dim and unseeing eyes.

Rebecca sunk down to kneel at the bed, as, one by one, the room emptied. Mrs. O'Reilly sat down beside her and placed a hand on her shoulder. The gesture offered little comfort. She was, at present, too shocked to shed tears, but she knew, somehow, she was to blame. She asked the question again.

"What happened?" It was merely a whisper, but it was loud enough for Mrs. O'Reilly.

"We found her at the bottom of the stairs. I think she must have been sleepwalking. Perhaps it was one of her night-mares. No one saw her. No one heard until it was too late. It wasn't your fault."

"Not my fault? The reason I sleep here is to keep her from having her nightmares. I stayed way last night. It was selfish of me. Wicked."

"It is not always wicked to be selfish. Not when one is so rarely so. And it was my fault if it was anyone's. I knew what she needed, but she fell asleep before I retired."

Rebecca saw the tears in the woman's eyes, and they were clearly not the first she had shed that day. Mrs. O'Reilly pulled her near and held her as, at last, her own tears came. "You did all you could for her. More than anyone else would ever have done, or could ever do."

"To what end?"

"To the end that she did not die friendless, and has left this cruel world for the comfort of a gentler one. She'll have no more nightmares, no more terrors and tremors. No fears, no pain."

This was some comfort, and yet... "We'll have a proper service for her. No unmarked pauper's grave."

Mrs. O'Reilly did not answer.

"I have some money. It will cover the expense."

"Rebecca—"

She had begun her protest, but Rebecca would not hear it. "I must. I'll never be able to forgive myself if I'm not allowed to honor her, to remember her, as she ought to be remembered."

Mrs. O'Reilly thought for a moment, and then, at last, nodded her head and held Rebecca close once more.

* * *

Rebecca stood just within the park gate. From here she could see the house and the road at once. Zachary was late. She was not terribly surprised, for she knew extricating him from Bentlow farm would be a particular difficulty on this day, even with the Squire's help.

She felt no impatience, no urgency in respect to the day's mission. As important as it was, she had other matters on her mind. Adelaide had been laid to rest. A beautiful if humble stone marked the spot. A little of that guilt she felt, and perhaps would always feel, had been eased. Mrs. O'Reilly had been right. She had gone to a better place. Had found rest, at long last, and where better than with her Maker? And now, with Adelaide gone, with today's mission before her, she saw no reason to remain with the Sisters at all. If today should prove a success—or even if it should prove a failure—she could not go back. What she was to do from this day forth she had put in God's hands.

Contemplating Arthur Tremonton's palatial manor house once more, she wondered what God had in mind for him. She thought she knew. It was why she was here, after all. And yet each man had his choice to follow the plans made for him, or to resist them, as Mr. Tremonton had done all his life so far. Was it his wealth that had made him so stubborn and proud? What would have become of him had he been born a pauper? She knew the answer already. His life would have been filled with difficulty and trial. He might have died on the streets, or worse, in a workhouse such as that from which the Sisters had rescued Zachary. It was impossible not to compare the two men. They could not be more different. The only thing they shared in common was a striking likeness, though Zachary was strong and fit (he necessarily had to be), while Mr. Tremonton was rather thin and frail from long years of idleness. Even in manner and temperament they were miles apart. But was it the money alone that made the difference? For all her efforts, she could not imagine Zachary as a cruel man with few principles outside of those dictated by pride. But then Zachary had submitted to his lot, whereas Mr. Tremonton fought it day in and day out, bitter that his money had failed in restoring that to him which was free to the common man.

"I still don't know how you did it," Zachary said, appearing suddenly at her side. She had been so engrossed in her own thoughts she had not heard him approach. It was as though it were she who were deaf today. As if one man's malady could be visited upon another, his afflictions and weaknesses traded. If only it were so. Well...the day was still young.

"Are you going to tell me how you accomplished it?"

She looked at him, and remembering herself and her reasons for bringing him, she smiled. "I'm entitled to my secrets."

"For now," he said and smiled. "So this is it, is it?"

She turned back toward the house and contemplated it a moment longer. "This is it."

"Shall we go in? Or did you only require that I stand here and gape at the house. It's an easy enough request." He examined it for a moment, then: "Done. Can we go now?" Teasing, he turned back to the road.

"Come," she said, and took his arm.

Together they moved forward along the path, neither speaking until they had arrived at the door. Rebecca reached for the knocker, but Zachary forestalled her.

"Let me," he said, and took the iron ring in his hand, striking it hard against the great oaken door.

They waited. Of course they waited.

"Are you certain they're expecting us?"

She was conscious then that she had not properly pre-pared him for this.

"There is something I possibly should tell you," she said. "The position I spoke of, it isn't, so to speak, open."

"I don't understand."

"It's true that Mr. Tremonton is in need of someone to serve him as a companion, only..."

"Only?"

"Well, he's not yet conscious of his need."

Zachary laughed stiffly. "Just what have you gotten me into, Miss Adair?"

"Be brave. All will be well."

"If that is so, then why do you look so extraordinarily pale?"

She didn't know how to answer this, and was rescued from the need by the opening of the door.

"You again?" the valet asked with an exceedingly furtive glance in Rebecca's direction. And then, observing Zachary, backlit by the sun and casting him in silhouette. "You've brought a friend, have you?"

"This is the Brother I spoke of. This is Zachary Good-fellow."

Zachary, thus introduced, stepped out of Rebecca's shad-ow. The valet-cum-butler blinked and looked more closely, then stepped back, his eyes wide. "Good God! What have you done?"

"I believe Mr. Tremonton is expecting us," she said.

Thompson looked askance, then more pointedly at Zachary. He looked to Rebecca, though briefly, then into the entrance hall and back at Zachary before slowly standing aside to allow them entrance. "Just... w-wait here." He examined Zachary a moment more and shuffled off to announce the visitors, and to enquire as to whether they would be received.

* * *

In Mr. Tremonton's upstairs receiving room, Zachary stood at Rebec-ca's side.

"You are a woman of your word, it seems," Mr. Tremonton observed gravely to Rebecca and ignoring Zachary entirely.

"I am, sir," she answered him.

"And I am a man of my word. I will not receive him."

Rebecca, half-abashed, looked to Zachary. He gave her a blank look in return, revealing nothing of what he really thought or felt. He was not certain he yet knew.

"We have come, Mr. Tremonton," she said, addressing him once more. "Whether you wish it or not, we have come. Perhaps it would be wise not to waste time with foolish obstinacies."

"It's not *my* time you waste, Miss Adair. And if *yours* is wasted, that is the price you pay for imposing yourself on others. I don't know what it is you want."

"I don't want for myself, sir. I told you that I believe you are in want of a companion."

"Him?" he said with a scoffing laugh. "This mouth-breathing oaf?"

Rebecca looked once more to Zachary. It was harder, this time, to conceal his irritation. She turned back to Mr. Tremonton. "Yes, sir," she answered.

"Is *he* mute, as well?"

"No, sir."

"Why does he not speak?"

"Because you have not addressed him, I believe."

"He is not deaf?"

"He *is* deaf, sir."

"He is blind, I think you said. Or was."

"He is partially blind, sir, yes."

"And his recovery..." He waved in obscure circles before him, gesturing toward what he could not see. "You are not responsible?"

"No, sir."

"And so what use have I for a half blind, apparently mute and admittedly deaf companion? How are we to communicate?"

"He understands you, sir."

"How?"

"He can see your mouth, read the movements of your lips. He can interpret your speech. And your intentions, I believe."

Mr. Tremonton raised his eyebrows. "Do you understand me, Mr. Goodfellow?"

"I do, sir."

"And what do you think of your friend's orchestrations on your behalf? No doubt you are grateful for the opportunity to gain such a potentially lucrative position."

"There's been no talk of money, sir. And hardly any of obtaining the position in question. I was only asked to meet you, and now I have. As far as I'm concerned, my object here is finished."

This seemed to pull Mr. Tremonton up. He sat more rigidly in his chair and leaned forward a little. "And if I dis-miss you this instant?"

"I will go and gladly."

Mr. Tremonton looked vaguely impressed. "He is better prepared than you to do all he is asked," he said to Rebecca as if this were a lesson she might take to heart. "You do not want this position, then?" he asked Zachary next.

"I have a position already, sir, and one that I'm not keen to give up."

"It pays you well?"

"Well enough."

"Which wages you hand over to the Bentlows," Rebecca added.

"Who are these Bent-lows?"

"They are the kind farmer, and his wife, who have raised me and brought me up to appreciate my good fortune," Zachary answered.

"Good fortune? You are deaf and half blind, man! What fortune is there in that?"

"I have work. I have the respect of those around me. And despite what it may appear," he said with a meaningful glance at Rebecca, "I can come and go as I wish. I can leave the Bentlows when I like, Miss Adair, you know that."

"I do know it, Mr. Goodfellow."

"You are free," Mr. Tremonton observed thoughtfully. "And yet you choose to stay where you are?"

"There is much good I can do there. And my life, though not easy, has done much to shape me into the man I am and hope one day to become. I'm glad to have learned to work for my bread, to till the ground, to look after the animals, to read and to speak, even to see. And to appreciate these as God's gifts, none of which He owed me. And all of which being more than I deserve, I mean to repay Him, where and how I can. It is clear I cannot do that here."

"Is it, now? I think your friend thinks differently. Just what was it you had in mind for him, Miss Adair?"

"I had hoped he would teach you that you might be happy despite your deficiencies. That a life spent in the service of others, not dwelling on that which has been denied you, is the answer to living a life of fulfillment."

"You compare us?"

"I do."

"That is absurd! I am blind. He is not."

"He was."

"He is a pauper, a deaf, uneducated pauper."

"You fail to see him correctly."

"I don't have to stand for this, sir." And Zachary turned to leave the room. But he stopped again. He could not leave Rebecca. Not with the likes of this man, whoever he was or might presume to be. He placed himself before the fire and waited, though not quite patiently, for Rebecca to finish her business. From here he could see what she said. He did not care to look upon Mr. Tremonton again. The sight of the man repulsed him.

"He says he's free!" Tremonton went on. "He is free now that he has had a part of his sight restored. I have not been given that. How can a man be free who cannot see where he goes or how to get there?"

"Zachary has learned to see in other ways. To feel and to understand his surroundings in ways most could never begin to understand. He has had his talents alone to rely upon. As a poor man, he did not have wealth as you have to assist him."

"I'm to feel pity for him, then, am I?"

"No, sir. You are to envy him."

"Envy him? *Him?*" Mr. Tremonton said and pointed at nothing.

"Can you leave your fine house, Mr. Tremonton? Or has it not become a prison to you? Zachary, though he works for his living, has friends in high places, friends who will vouch for him, who will provide for him in time of need. He can go where he likes. Rich or poor, he has friends. Have you freedom, Mr. Tremonton? Have you friends?"

"I have precisely what I need," he answered somewhat resignedly. "No less, and no more."

"So the answer, then, is no."

Mr. Tremonton grumbled and shifted positions in his chair.

"My friend, Mr. Goodfellow, might teach you a great deal about independence. He might help you to gain a better understanding of the world around you, give you the chance to live life as you've never lived it, rather than sitting here alone, a prisoner of it."

"And what, exactly, must I do in return?"

"All you have to do is open your mind to new experiences. You have to want to see, not with your eyes, but with your other senses, with other parts of your understanding. You have to want to see the world as it truly is. Do you?"

He thought for a very long time. No doubt the idea of escaping the confines of this house, to experience just a little of what he had learned of with the help of others, to learn things for himself quite independent of that help, appealed to him. For the briefest moment it appeared that Mr. Tremonton was considering. Considering very carefully, and then...

"What I want, Miss Adair, is to have my sight restored. Your friend cannot do that for me, can he?"

"No. I'm afraid he cannot. No one can."

"You can."

Rebecca took a step back. Zachary took a step toward her and stopped. She looked to him, a little afraid it seemed, then steadied herself, holding up a hand to stay him as well. If she was feigning courage

35

for his benefit, he'd have something to say to her about it later. But there was only one way to know what she was being made to endure. He looked to Mr. Tremonton once more.

"Come here, girl," he said to her. "Come here, I say!"

"You needn't," Zachary assured her, then, turning to Mr. Tremonton: "You will speak respectfully to Miss Adair, sir."

"Yes, yes, very well!" Tremonton said and took a breath to calm himself. His face was red, and he was growing increasingly excited. "Come, Miss Adair, would you please indulge me?" Tremonton's manner was simpering now, and it grated much worse than had his disrespectful demands. "Come, come, come."

As she approached Mr. Tremonton, he reached out and snatched her hands in his. He removed her gloves and threw them to the floor. Her hands were tightly fisted as he held her by the wrists.

So Tremonton knew of her strange gift. And he wanted it. Of course he wanted it for himself. "Release her, if you please!" Zachary said and approached him.

"Before I make up my mind about you, sir," Tremonton said, addressing him, "I'd like to see you for myself. If you don't mind."

Zachary looked to Rebecca and waited. She gave a silent nod. This, it seemed, was a part of her plan, yet she did not look pleased by the prospect of it. He feared he knew why. He feared more that she would be proved right. But, obedient to her desire, still confused by her design, he took a step back and watched. Carefully.

Tremonton raised her fisted hands to his face, where she slowly uncurled her fingers to place over his eyes. He held them there. Then, slowly, very slowly, her fingers slid down his eyelids. When they were uncovered, he looked, and he looked long.

At last he blinked. "You are a fine looking young man. I'm glad to know it."

"It is not the most significant of his qualities," Rebecca said.

Tremonton's gaze shifted to her face. He blinked again and winced, and would have let her go were it not for the risk of losing his sight once more.

"A woman like you would make much of him, I suppose."

"I do," she said, though very quietly. But Zachary heard it. And it made it all the harder to watch her held in this man's hungry grasp.

"You have never seen your own face, Mr. Tremonton," she said now. "Perhaps you would like to."

His eyes widened at the prospect never before thought of (or possible) and nodded.

"Perhaps your valet would be good enough to fetch a mirror."

The man, who had been present, if silent, this whole time, now left to retrieve the requested object. He returned a moment later and held it before Mr. Tremonton, who, apparently amazed, freed one hand and began exploring his face with his fingers, as if comparing the sensation of those familiar features against the vision that was wholly unfamiliar to him. He was clearly pleased by what he saw. He smiled, then looked once more to Zachary. The smile faded. His brow furrowed. His mouth twitched uncomfortably.

Once more he turned to the mirror, and then back up at his valet. "Is it my imagination, Thompson, or does Miss Adair's companion not bear a slight resemblance to me?"

Thompson appeared afraid to answer.

"Why do you hesitate, man? Does he or does he not look a little like me?"

"The resemblance, sir, is striking."

"No one asked my opinion, but I do not see a resemblance in the slightest," Zachary answered. And he didn't. But then he wouldn't, for his sight did not work like that of other men. He did not understand how this frail, hollow and biting creature could be thought to bear any remarkable likeness to himself. They each had a head, two legs and two arms. And that, Zachary felt, was where the similarities ended.

"Miss Adair," Tremonton said next, without looking at her, "what is your opinion?"

"You do look alike, sir. And there is a reason for it."

Tremonton suddenly looked pale, and something hard and unsettling descended upon Zachary.

"What is this, Miss Adair?" Tremonton demanded of her. "What have you done? Tell me I do not know this man."

"You do not know him, sir."

"Tell me I *should* not know him. That there is no reason for me to know him."

Zachary watched, willing Rebecca to answer, and to do it just as she was asked to do. She did not. In fact she remained quite silent. A look of regret flashed across her face as she looked to him, and then looked quickly away again.

"Do you know me?" Tremonton demanded of Zachary.

"I do not, sir. Nor am I likely to want to."

Mr. Tremonton, still holding Rebecca's wrist, gave it a great tug and pulled her near. The mirror dropped to the ground and broke into several pieces at her feet.

Zachary stepped forward as Rebecca stifled a cry. The valet alone, with a hand on his arm, prevented him from seizing hold of the man.

"What is it you want, Miss Adair?" Tremonton demanded of her now. "What is it you have come for? Have you come to see me humiliated? Shamed? Embarrassed?"

"Of course not, sir. I only meant to help you if I could. To offer friendship. You are in need of it, whether or not you want to admit it."

"I do not want *him*! Why did you bring *him*?"

"I told you. You needed a brother."

There was a humming silence, and then: "I thought you meant a Brother from one of your confounded charity societies!"

"I did not say so, sir. You are hurting me. Please, let me go."

Zachary took another step forward, but the valet held tighter. Tremonton eased his grip on Rebecca, though he did not release her. He would hold onto her, it seemed, until the end of his life. Or hers.

"I'll ask you once to let the lady go," Zachary said, throwing the valet off and in a tone that could brook no argument.

"Lady? Lady? This woman?" Tremonton laughed. "Your eyesight is poor indeed if you think of her as a lady. Have you seen her face?"

Tremonton turned her around to face Zachary. He beheld what he always beheld, but as if in concentrated form. A wo-man ashamed of what she could not help, patient in the face of trial and hardship, courageous in the face of cruelty. She did not deserve this.

"I see someone good and beautiful, kind and virtuous. Someone far above you, sir. Release her this minute."

But she was as tarnished gold in Tremonton's hand. It did not please him, but neither would he release it. He would not lose what she alone could give him.

Zachary shrugged off the valet, stepped forward, and collared Tremonton, who instantly released her and then, his gaze resting solidly on Zachary's, held it there until the last remnants of Rebecca's gift faded from his eyes.

"We are brothers," Tremonton said, as if just now realizing the truth of it.

"We may be, for all I know. But I'll not acknowledge you as kin."

Tremonton appeared relieved, and Zachary released his hold, pushing him away. Tremonton's courage seemed to return now along

38

with his color as he sat, slack and slouching in his comfortable chair. Yet Zachary remained where he stood, planted firmly between Rebecca and their reluctant host.

"I think we'll go now," Zachary said, but the reply was not what he had expected.

"What happened to her?" Tremonton asked of him.

"That is for Miss Adair to tell, though you've no right to ask."

"Tell me," he said, turning to her. "I beg of you."

Rebecca approached Mr. Tremonton once more, stopping to stand beside Zachary. She examined the glass that lay in large shards upon the floor. She stooped to take one up, and stood, examining it for a moment or two. At last she spoke, if weakly. "I was not wanted," she said, "by my father or any-one. Perhaps you'll understand the feeling, Mr. Tremonton. He wished to be rid of me. One night, in an apoplexy of drink and opium, he thought to take my life. He was not fit for the task. He left me as you see me now."

"I don't see you, if you recall," he answered her bitterly. "If you would—"

"I won't, sir. It was not me you were meant to see. But yourself. And your brother. But you refused to see him, even to receive him. You will not acknowledge him. Is it too late? Will you not let him help you?"

"How is he to help *me*? I don't believe that was your plan at all. You want *me* to help *him*, admit it."

"Perhaps I thought you could help each other. You might help him to have the opportunities so unjustly denied him. He can help you to rise above your affliction. To make the most of your challenges and turn them into blessings."

They were silent again for a time. Tremonton seemed to be considering once more Rebecca's words, struggling as he did between feelings of hope and despair, possibility and resentment. And then something seemed to come over him. A calmness. A decision. An idea?

"I will acknowledge him," Tremonton said, sitting straighter.

"You will?"

"I do not care to be acknowledged, sir."

"Zachary, please," she said. "Listen to him."

"I want to see again. And you can grant me that, Miss Adair. I will acknowledge him if you will stay and be my eyes. Keep them open. He will be my brother if you will restore my sight."

"It is not so easy as that, Mr. Tremonton. Were I to restore your sight, you would still be blind in the most significant of ways. Don't you see that it requires some sacrifice?"

But the sacrifice, it seemed was to be all on her side. At least Tremonton would have it so.

"*You* can see. *He* can see!" he shouted. "And you can help me to see! Why won't you do it? You have come to help! And yet you refuse at the same time! You taunt me, Miss Adair. And yet I will have what you offer!"

Rebecca took a step back as Mr. Tremonton rose from his chair. Zachary remained standing between them as she backed slowly from the room. The valet looked on, paralyzed it seemed.

"Where are you?" Tremonton demanded. "Come here. Stay with me. I'll give you anything. Anything you want! With you I could live a normal life. I could marry you, to make it right and proper. You would be grateful, I dare say, to have a husband."

"Not any husband, sir."

"I would not be unkind."

"Only selfish."

Tremonton took another step forward and Zachary laid a hand on his chest to stop him. He did stop, but otherwise paid him no mind. He saw what he wanted to see, felt what he wanted to feel, and nothing more.

"We are all selfish, Miss Adair," he argued. "You as well as I. Is it not selfishness that brings you here now? And you are not so difficult to look upon. You were clearly quite pretty once. A veil, I think, would cover the worst of it and—"

But Arthur Tremonton got no further, for it was then that Zachary struck him. Tremonton fell to the ground, dazed, but looked up at Zachary. For a moment it seemed he recognized him. He held a hand out to him as his gaze fixed solidly upon him.

Rebecca's hand was suddenly in Zachary's, tugging him away, toward the door. It was time to go.

"Good day to you, sir," Zachary said. "We'll not trouble you again."

Whatever focus Tremonton had briefly gained by the blow, he seemed to lose again. He curled himself up in a ball and let out a long and mournful wail. And the sound, desperate, devouring, unholy, did not cease until Zachary and Rebecca left the house and were some distance from it. It was not a sound Zachary was grateful to have heard. It was not a sound he was likely to forget. But it was soon enough and mercifully replaced with the sound of birds chirping, of footsteps on stony earth, of a brook nearby.

It was only then that he realized he was no longer holding Rebecca's hand. Hers was now occupied in wiping the tears from her eyes, while the other held still to the shard of glass. Her gift, for the moment, lingered on.

With a hand on her arm, he turned her to him.

"I'm sorry," she said looking at him. "I don't know what I was thinking dragging you there."

"Why didn't you tell me?" Zachary asked her. "Why didn't you tell me I had a brother?"

"I couldn't have you accused of any mercenary motives. That was for me, not you."

"Mercenary? To try to change a man's life for the better?"

"He didn't want it, did he?"

Zachary paused a moment before answering. "No," he said, "but that does not diminish the value of the gift you offered him."

"It *is* diminished. It hurt you, and I am sorry."

She looked at him a moment longer and then turned to walk on. In silence, he followed. But the silence, now, was too much to bear. If ever there was a time for speech, for confession, it was now. He took her hand once more and stopped. He held it a moment, just held it, looked at it as he stroked the back of it with his thumb.

"You also hoped," he said at last, "that he would make something of me. Something more than I already am."

"I hoped he would be grateful. That you might gain what you ought to have had, had pride and avarice not run so strongly in your father's heart."

"And what did you hope for yourself?" he asked, looking up from her hand to her flushed and tear-stained face.

"I suppose..."

"Go on."

"I suppose I thought...if you were free to do and live as you wished, if you were truly at liberty, then, well...I might be too. One day."

"Oh, Rebecca," he said, and released her hand so he could touch his own to her face. "Don't you know that was what Squire Humphrey meant to do for us all along?"

"What?" she said and the tears started anew. She looked down at the shard of glass she still held in the other hand.

41

"This mirror," he said, taking it from her, "is not always honest. We look into it to see ourselves, and what is reflected back is an image we think we understand. I sometimes think I can see myself better in it with my bad eye than with my good."

She shook her head and turned from him.

"I want you to look into it," he said, placing it in her hand. "I want you to try to see what I see. Do you think you can?"

"How can I?"

"Just try it, will you? Look."

He raised her hand and held it as it held the glass, just before her face so that she could see only the side without the scar. She looked, smiled slightly and looked at him. Gently he guided the mirror to reflect the other side of her face. Her gaze remained on him, until, at last, he nodded his encouragement and she looked. Her brow furrowed, her hand raised to trace the scar, as dark now as it had ever been.

"What I see is a woman—a beautiful, good and worthy woman—who has fought with the world and won. A soldier coming home from the fight, bearing no scars, cannot have done much fighting. Did he hide in the barracks? Run from battle? Our men come home bloodied and battered, and for a reason. Sometimes they are scarred more within than without. It's our imperfections that make us perfectly willing to accept all that God has in store for us. Somewhere in you, you know that. It's why I am who I am. It's what you hoped to show Arthur Tremonton. It's why your scar has never completely healed. It is why, when you touch me, I can hear, but I can see no better. I do not want to forget what I over-came. It has made me a better person."

He took the glass, threw it away into a ditch, where it shattered and sparkled in the sun. And then, without any warning, he drew her to him and kissed her once and well. He could hear and feel his blood pulsing, heard bells ringing, saw flashes of light in his blind eye and in his good. He held her to him a moment longer, and then, releasing her, though reluctantly, they made their way, hand in hand, not in silence, but with the happiness all the world had now to offer them buzzing around their heads.

* * *

It was a bright morning, and warm. Church bells rang in the distance. Thompson had heard there was to be a wedding in the village. It was the perfect day for it, too. Mr. Tremonton had been rather low of late. Since Miss Adair's visit, he had seemed a different man, sunken, spent. Thompson suspected it had something to do with her presumptuous and foolhardy decision to force Mr. Tremonton's younger brother before him. No doubt it had reawakened memories best forgotten. They had been recalled, it seemed, brought back to the fore by Miss Adair's visit and the strange spells she cast. Mr. Tre-monton had declared he had been able to see. It certainly appeared to have been so, but how could that be? She had played some trick on him; that was all. But whatever had happened, it had left Mr. Tremonton very low. Very low, indeed. It was almost as if he had become a sulky and petulant child all over again. As if someone had given him some great and rare toy, and then had taken it away. And, as a child would do, he had valued it beyond its worth. He did not seem to want to go on now, until he had his playthings returned to him. He had even declared he might be a little in love with Miss Adair, were she not so gruesome to look upon. Lovely, too, in her way, but gruesome. And interfering, which was the worst of curses any woman could visit upon a well-meaning husband. Mr. Tremonton would recover in time. And Thompson had a plan in mind to hurry that recovery along.

It being so glorious a day, he thought perhaps he might take his master out of doors, to sit in the garden, amidst the newly bloomed flowers, the sun shining and the soft wind blowing the gentle fragrance of apple blossoms and narcissus about. It was a sure way to cheer anyone's mood, however dark.

Thompson entered his master's room to find he was out of bed. Odd, he never rose on his own. But the window was open, and the breeze blowing gently through it. Yes, his plan was a good one, and Mr. Tremonton would thank him for it, too.

Thompson checked in the adjoining room, in the library and receiving room, in the dressing room. Mr. Tremonton was not there. Well, he must be somewhere.

"Mr. Tremonton," he called. "your breakfast is on its way. Where would you like me to set table?"

There was no answer.

A dog barked, then howled.

"That blasted mongrel is back, it seems," he said under his breath and opened the doors to the balcony to see for himself if the beast could be found. They'd driven it off before, though it had taken a week or so to persuade it that it was not wanted here. At last, it seemed, they had succeeded. And now this!

He heard the sound again, mournful and haunting. And closer this time. Near the house, perhaps? He examined the surrounding yard and saw nothing. Then he heard it again, closer than ever. He examined the pathways and gardens, and saw nothing. And then again, as if it were just below him, he heard it once more. He looked down, at the ground just below the balcony. Nothing. And the windows, the East first, nothing. Then the West. Something.

Dear heaven, was it possible?

He left the room, and entering the corridors called for help. The cook, housekeeper, the kitchen and laundry maids met him in the kitchen garden, and together they circled the house to examine the nearly indiscernible heap that lay beneath Mr. Tremonton's open window.

Indeed, it was Mr. Tremonton himself.

God in Heaven, what had he done? Had he fallen? By accident? Or was this something else?

"God rest his soul," said the cook.

"Poor unhappy fellow," said the laundry maid.

Mrs. Pritchett, teapot in hand, unwittingly emptied its contents on the grass and fell to her knees beside him, stricken, apparently, though he'd never spoken a civil word to her in his life.

In a daze, Thompson returned indoors, leaving the female staff to sniff and lament and conjecture on their own. What would happen to them now? Thompson had been a member of this household since Robert Tremonton was a child. Who would have the house, now? Who would be master? Anyone? No one? For Tremonton had no family. None at all.

Save one. A brother whom no one had recognized. Whom no one had wanted. But they were brothers. Thompson would attest to it. Yes. Yes, he would.

* * *

It is an undeniable irony of life that, despite his many hard-ships, man is often shaped and molded by misfortune. The poor man understands the pain of poverty, and when life, in its manifold mysteries and designs, grants him a fortune, he knows how best to use it.

The weather, as mundane a thing as can be imagined, yet blesses our lives, helping us through days filled with rain to appreciate all the more the shining of the sun as it kisses our skin and persuades the flowers to bloom.

Our five senses, likewise, are blessings for which we are ever grateful, all the more so when we have lived a portion of our lives without them. With eyes that have known what it is to see only darkness, one learns to look beyond the obvious. With ears that have known, if only for a time, a world cast in silence, one learns to rejoice in the everyday, to take joy in the mundane. A happy home is more desirable than an empty one, however stately it may be. A clever, selfless and loving woman, far more suitable than she who has only the pleasure of her appearance to offer.

In finding the hidden beauty, do we not often find that the physical becomes all the more attractive?

Perhaps.

Perhaps not.

* * *

In a small parish church in a quaint little village stands just such a couple as we might put these questions to. At the mo-ment we join them, we see that they are caught up in the excitement of the day. But this is only a part (though admit-tedly the greater part) of their joy. Other considerations circumstantially have added to them, for the weather is bright and warm, the breeze gentle and fresh. The flowers and blossoms are out in abundance, and the world appears new and promising.

* * *

By the witnesses that attend, the proudly smiling Mrs. O'Reilly among them, this couple might have been described, were you to ask them— and of course they would be inclined to oblige—as a couple of better than average compatibility, honest, good and humble.

The bride was young and beautiful. Exceedingly so, despite (or perhaps even because of) the pale scar that marked her fair face. The groom was handsome, well connected, with many friends if little family and more than ready to dote upon his new bride.

But what were they to live on, you might ask? And where and in what fashion? Fate provides the way for those prepared to follow the path made out for them by their Maker.

Squire Humphrey, a committed bachelor, was nevertheless lonely. He had not much to leave besides his great house and the land that surrounded it, but that was no matter. There was no debt to encumber it, and Mr. and Mrs. Goodfellow had no very great expectations.

And who was to say they might not, one day, come into some fortune?

Whether or not happiness would be their life long companion, there is no need to conjecture. I'll tell you, my friend. The answer is yes!

About the Author

V.R. Christensen is a native of Washington State but currently resides in southern Virginia where she writes about historic homes for OldWestEndVA.com, a historic preservation marketing initiative based out of Danville, Virginia. She's also a trauma-informed yoga instructor and founder of the community outreach program HAPI (the Health and Peace Initiative) which works to coordinate yoga, meditation, and holistic healing practices to the underserved.

About the Illustrator

After training in Classical and Early Music, B. Lloyd studied at the Accademia di Belle Arti di Venezia, where she graduated in 2005. She has taken part in art fairs and exhibitions in Italy and Holland, including the Ootmarsum Art Fairs and Wierden Art Events.

B. Lloyd is also a writer and the founder of Authors Anon, a venue where both published and non-published authors of high quality fiction can share their work and gain exposure.

B. Lloyd lives and works in Venice.

For more information about B. Lloyd and her work, please visit her at www.wix.com/artscribe/paintings.

www.ingramcontent.com/pod-product-compliance
Lightning Source LLC
Chambersburg PA
CBHW020651130626
46552CB00003B/1506